IF YA WANNA KNOW

IF YA WANNA KNOW

Original Songs and Links to YouTube Woven into a Story of Suspense

T. R. COMSTOCK

Published in the United States of America

ISBN: 978-1-64460-045-0 (*sc*)
      978-1-64460-044-3 (*e*)

Published by Stonewall Press
4800 Hampden Lane, Suite 200, Bethesda, MD 20814 USA
1.888.334.0980 | www.stonewallpress.com

1. Suspense
2. Literature
18.12.11

This is a story of how a few songs (words and links to YouTube included) finally made their legitimate discovery by the followers of country pop music. It follows the action of person, whose job is to uphold the law, that claims to be the author of original songs while believing that the true writer has succumbed to an auto accident. Although the true author is in a comatose state, he and his Fiancé struggle to maintain rightful ownership of the songs. It has an unusual beginning, but no more unusual than the personality of the song writer who is also a graduate student of engineering.

T R Comstock
tcomstock17@gmail.com

Contents

CHAPTER I

School Year Ends

SOMEONE ONCE SAID THAT the best song has not been heard by anyone but the old person in the mountains of Appalachia who wrote it. How a song comes about is a fascinating thought process? If it never becomes familiar to anyone else, it must have been worth the effort for someone to express a deep emotion. Let the adventure of one writer begin.

It is late spring. The air is fresh, the sky is a deep blue, unlike it has been since the days preceding early May. All students, undergraduate and graduate, at the University of Cincinnati are preparing for their final exams and their summer get away. The faculty, except those few who have summer assignments, are anticipating a break from their duties as well.

This activity is somewhat different for Mark Dawson of the Mechanical Engineering Department. He prepares to finish his proposal to the Material Air Command, Division of the US Air Force at Dayton, OH. He is searching for the funds that will allow him to implement and prove that his analysis of an electro-hydraulic vibration controller for machine tools is a practical solution to these production limiting problems. Equally important, this will allow Mark to complete his dissertation that is required for his PhD.

As he meets with the Department Chairman, Dr. John Wittig, the two engage in hopeful conversation regarding the project that

Mark is proposing. Dr. Wittig laments that it will be fall before any news will be forthcoming about the acceptance of the proposal and asks Mark if he has plans for the summer. "Oh, I intend to use the time to promote a few songs that I have worked out and recorded with some of the guys that I bang around with and share my interest in music." Dr. Wittig remarks that "it is good that you have other interest than just engineering. If a person wants to describe bad art, they say it is mechanical, if they want to describe bad music, they say it is mechanical, if they want to describe bad love making, they say it is mechanical. So what do they call us? Mechanical Engineers!" The two share a good laugh.

As you know," Mark continues, "my father's burial site is located in Camp Nelson outside of Lexington, KY. He was buried at the Camp in honor of being a veteran of the Korean War. So I intend to visit his site on the way down to Nashville. Thanks for your support Dr. Wittig, and I'll keep in touch to see if you hear anything from the Air Force. If not, I'll see you this Fall and we can pursue the project as best we can until funds are available."

Mark leaves the Chairman's office and returns to the graduate room. This room is not fancy but it is located off the main laboratory that houses all the equipment that is available for the completion of ongoing projects. There are several personal computers in the graduate room that provide the necessary software for testing and analysis, most of which have been developed by grad students within the department. At this time Mark is only interested in using one of the many phones that are available to the students. He calls his future wife, Lora Burton, to confirm their get together at the "Homestead Bar & Grill" this evening.

CHAPTER II

Last Jam Session

Lora and Mark have been together for the past two years. She is a student at UC's Conservatory of Music and, like Mark, hopes to earn her PhD within the next few years. Her goal is to become a teacher in the music department of a prominent university. The two, known as L&M, have been going to the Homestead, which is located just a few miles away from the campus, for the past year.

The Homestead is owned and operated by Vic and Dorothy Lynge and features live country music. This old bar and grill, established in the 30's, who's hay day past when lunch was no longer a necessity to the laid off workers at the Trailmobile and Kenner Toy manufacturing plants. "Open mike" nights are the most important to L&M since they, and his buddies, have been recording Mark's original songs. This will be Mark's last night and he will be completing a series of songs that began when they started frequenting the bar.

Lora's job is to perform the songs that Mark feels is more appropriate for the female artist. She has a very pleasant voice and L&M perform Mark's songs as well as they do their serious work at the university.

As the band prepares to perform, Mark grabs the mike and comments that he is a long way from his childhood mountain home in Peach Creek, WV. I recall, he announces, "that my Grandfather would play the banjer claw hammer style and sing old railroad songs. Those were the days." He then adds that, "my new song, "It's After Midnight, is a little different than the songs of my Grandfather. It goes like this,"

> [1]It's after midnight, your gone all day I'm gettin' uptight
> Where the lights are dim
> I know you're out with him, or maybe his place
> Were he looks down and smiles on your face
> And makin' love to the one, that should be here at home
> I'm not the kind of man to live a life like this
> I don't need the kind of love Who'd steal another's kiss
>
> Won't give you my name, while you go on and play your fools game
> You better make it last, it'll soon be in my past
> There is no new day, our love is gone I know there's no way
> So give it babe your all, I hope you have a ball
> I'm not the kind of man who'll let you bring him down
> I'm not the kind of man who'll always be around
> 1. URL (https://youtu.be/dZa37545MQw) "It's After Midnight"
>
> Don't come back pleading, another's love I know your needing
> You will find what is right, by then the morning's light
> Will cast my shadow, as I go walking through the meadow
> And when you wonder why, don't say I didn't try
> I'm not the kind of man to spend a lot of time
> To get someone like you to see, when I know your blind
> It's after midnight, (pause) It's after midnight, (pause) it's after midnight

The audience stands and applauds in response to Marks's performance, and he thanks the crowd and realizes that his song will be well received if he can get it public exposure.

Lora is now asked to take the mike and sing the last song to be recorded before Mark leaves town for the summer. Lora tells the audience that she has selected a song that Mark wrote for her in their early days. She continues to address the crowd, "it is entitled Time Will Tell," and begins to sing.

> [1]When we first met, love's fire hadn't yet started burning
> Together we strolled down love ol' road ever turning
> But love said go on, don't be alone and remember
> A love with a past is a love that will last and fulfill.
>
> The passing of time will tell me if I'm really needing
> A heart such as yours, a love that endures and believing
> That our love will grow and I'll always know you are near me
> Till then we'll sing and our love will bring what it may
>
> Until the years have proved that our tears won't be falling
> And loves second glance has proved there's a chance I'll be calling
> On you to remain and always unchanged in your feelings
> That our futures light will be just as bright as today.

Again, the audience applauds and Lora senses that Mark has proven his ability to please a crowd with a song. Of course, her performance certainly supported Mark's writing talent.

After the performances, Mark has the unpleasant task of saying goodbye to Lora. He explains that he must make an effort to get his songs published and presented professionally to the general public. Although he is lacking the funds to be on the road, he will do his best to complete his mission. As he says goodbye to Lora and his friends, he begins his trip by hitchhiking to Nashville by way of Lexington. This is Mark's last evening in Cincinnati.

1. URL (https://youtu.be/yqOMJ3oYgN4) "Time Will Tell"

CHAPTER III

First Visit to Nashville

U NDERSTANDING MARK'S CONNECTION TO Nashville is to understand his consulting project that took place in nearby Tullahoma some months ago. It all began when the Director of Industrial Research of the Mechanical Engineering Department invited Mark to meet in his office. The DIR explained that a local company shipped a rotary machine to the US Air Force at the base in Tullahoma. The prototype machine past all tests before it was shipped, but the engineers at the base claim that excessive vibration that occurs at the machine's rotating speed are unacceptable. The company wants a research crew to visit the site and determine the cause of the excessive vibration. After all, the machine represents a significant investment and the rejection of future orders by the Air Force is out of the question. As Mark leaves the office he is reminded by a plague on the DIR's wall that reads "We Get Too Soon Oldt, and Too Late Schmart."

Mark and his friend, Rocky, load the rental truck and arrive in Tullahoma ahead of the rest of the crew. The test equipment is set up and arrangements are made for everyone to be housed at the local motel.

The rest of the crew arrives and vibration testing of the machine begins. However, the efforts made in next few days does not reveal the cause of the problem. Since it has been connected to an air supply, it is impossible to take measurements of the internal parts of the machine. Failure seems to be snatched from the jaws of victory. The crew decide that the data must be taken back to the lab in Cincinnati in order to be examined more closely. Most of the crew will return home and leave Mark and Rocky to pack up and drive the truck back to the university. The two are now left alone to clean up.

Disheartened, Mark decides to forget everything he knows about vibration testing and just feel the machine, with the attached air supply, in operation. He calls Rocky over and asks, "do you feel that there is a difference between the movement at the transition of the machine and the air supply?" Rocky agrees and the measurement of motion is repeated, but this time the air supply is disconnected.

Low and behold, the excessive vibration no longer exists at the speed of rotation. Mark and Rocky now know that the gasket used to attach the air supply is acting as a flexible spring and causing the problem.

They report the findings to one of the engineers in charge of the machine. The engineer asks Mark if they can be present to observe their findings before the test equipment is loaded onto the truck. As other employees of the base are notified to attend the final tests, the measurements are repeated with and without the air supply attached. There, for all to see, is the proof that it is not the machine that is the problem but the attached air supply is like the tail wagging the dog.

Mark and Rocky decide to celebrate their victory by stopping in Nashville on the way back home. After all, it is getting late in the day and these tired heroes could use a night in a cool motel room. This doesn't mean that some night time activity is not in order. The guys use the facilities of the motel to freshen up and head out in a rental car.

The two have heard about the Red Fox Inn, which has open mike nights, and Mark wants to try a song that he has written for a friend. The friend has gone through a divorce and often relates to Mark how he has been effected by this traumatic event.

At the Inn, a few drinks will give Mark the courage to get up at the mike. He states, "This is a song about the aftermath of being divorced." He begins to sing his song entitled "Divorced and Free."

[1]"I had a wife and two good kids, and stayed home every night
But we gave up the ol' late show and started in to fight
She through me out, I'm here to say and now I'm runnin' roun'
And I know every by their first name every country band in town Chorus:
Divorced and free, liberty, this life is killin' me
I'm staying out every night, I'm up till' way past three
Someday I may remarry, and maybe settle down
Until then I'm gonna be in every swingin' place in town

My boss told me I'd lose my job, someday I might get fired
He said you've been moppin' round, and lately just to tired.
Each day I sit and hold my head, each night I'm runnin' free
I've sent the alimony, there's nothing left for me

I feel so disorganized, my clothes piled in the car
I'd leave this town tomorrow, but I wouldn't get too far
The food I eat it ain't the best, but it'll have to do
I'd die of malnutrition, before goin' back to you"

Mark steps down from the stage as the crowd applauses.

Meanwhile, Rocky has sweet talked a local girl and her sister into sharing a few dances with the boys. As the evening winds down, the girls volunteer to drive to their respective apartments. The guys only recall being driven down Broadway and smoke rising from the road due to the driver slamming the brakes hard to stop at each red light. Rocky says, "I can see the headlines in the paper, Two University Students Killed in Nashville."

In spite of the reckless driving, the boys make it back to the motel. The celebration is over and the heroes head back to Cincinnati the following morning to report their success.

1. URL (https://youtu.be/Q7f29Kpmcbo) "Divorced and Free"

———

CHAPTER IV

On to Music City

MARK, CARRYING ONLY HIS back pack filled with a change of clothes, a few snacks and his recordings, catches his first ride that takes him south on I-75 towards Lexington. The driver asks him where he's heading and the purpose of his trip. Mark tells him of his proposal to the Air Force and that he wants to promote his music in the meantime. "It seemed logical to take my recordings to Nashville" Mark says. He continues, "I have made arrangements to have an agent to hawk my songs to various producers." He mentions, as he did to Dr. Wittig, that a stopover to visit his Father's gravesite at Camp Nelson is also a priority.

Mark tells the driver, "my Dad had a great sense of humor. I recall his favorite story about a girl who kept trying to get some guy to marry her. The guy would say, what will we live on? The girls reply was we'll live on love. After the girl continued to ask for a commitment to marry and insisting they would live on love, the guy finally gave in. Following the hasty marriage and the first night of love making, the girl awoke, turned to the guy and said, I'm hungry!" The driver's laughter indicated that he enjoyed the story as they rode along. They continued to engage in typical conversation until they reach the outskirts of Lexington. Mark thanked the driver for the lift and says he will make the remaining leg to Camp Nelson on his own. Which he does.

He locates the gravesite of his Father, which is nestled under a large tree. It is a peaceful location and it pleases Mark. He talks to his Dad, Glen, and assures Glen that he will continue to complete his education. He explains to his Dad, "the trip to Nashville is mainly to satisfy my interest in music while I await word concerning my proposal." "It doesn't hurt to have options"

Mark leaves Camp Nelson and continues his journey to Nashville. Another stroke of luck allows him to catch a ride that takes him South on I-65 to Millersville, TN. This is a small town that is just outside of Nashville and not too far from his Aunt Hazel's home. Mark has made arrangements to stay at her place, which is in the heart of the city, and use it as a base from which to operate.

As the ride approaches Millersville it begins to rain heavily and darkness is near. Mark is left beside the road on highway 31W to make his way into town. The rain continues to fall even harder and it is almost dark as Mark attempts to hitch another ride to complete his trip into Nashville.

CHAPTER V

The Accident

A COMING CAR, WHICH IS traveling too fast for the rainy conditions and darkness, knocks Mark violently to the side of the road. As he lays near the roadside, the contents of his back pack is thrown all around his motionless body. Within about 15 minutes, Jeff Adkins, a Deputy Sheriff, passes by and spots Mark laying helpless by the road. The Deputy examines the body and is not sure if it has survived the accident. He thinks to himself, this is the guy that performed at the Red Fox Inn a few months ago. Then Jeff notices the recordings that have fallen from the back pack and he sees that they are marked as "master recordings-original songs." He decides to gather up the recordings and see if they can be used to support his own ambition to become a songwriter/performer. Of course, the Deputy must do his duty and call for an ambulance. However, Jeff must keep his secret about the recordings until the severity of Mark's accident is revealed.

The ambulance delivers Mark to the emergency ward of General Hospital where he is in critical condition. He is diagnosed as being in a coma due to having traumatic head injury. In addition, he has a few broken bones and he is assigned a private room until someone can be contacted to explain the circumstances surrounding this stranger's history.

Mark's Student ID provides his connection to the University of Cincinnati and Dr. Wittig's Department. Dr. Wittig in turn contacts Lora, whom he has meet in previous social gatherings, and explains the situation. Lora indicates that she will require a few days before she can be released from her duties at the conservatory. After all, Lora must monitor and grade the final exams for the classes that she has taught this spring. She begins to make plans to be at Mark's bedside as soon as possible because she has no idea of how long Mark will remain in his comatose state.

The Red Fox Inn

THE RED FOX INN is the hot spot in Nashville. Everyone that is seeking to fulfill their dream of becoming a country-pop star hangs out at the Inn. The Inn is the major league of country music as compared to the bush league status of the Homestead in Cincinnati. Open mike nights attract the "wanabes" and those looking to promote them. This is the spot that Deputy Sheriff, Jeff Adkins frequents and dreams of becoming a successful singer/writer. This is also where he witnessed Mark's past performance.

Jeff's visits to the Red Fox are often accompanied by his girlfriend, Ruth Beckman, an RN at the General Hospital in Nashville. Ruth is a diehard fan of country music and supports Jeff's aspirations of becoming a performer. Moreover, Ruth's position as a nurse at the General Hospital will play an important role in connecting L&M to Jeff's secret plot. She has already informed Jeff about a stranger who has been recently brought to the emergency ward as the result of an accident. Ruth tells Jeff, "It is very doubtful if this person will survive." This remark fuels Jeff's plans to proceed with his secret plot.

For now, Jeff and Ruth are attending the show at the Red Fox. A female is introduced by the MC and approaches the mike. She begins to sing a song that is announced as "Too Tired Tonight." She begins to sing about the detriment that work has on a woman's libido.

[1]"I know you need your woman to lay down by your side
To comfort and to give you the things that I provide
I hate to disappoint you but I'd like to get some sleep
I hope you kill the light dear and start in counting sheep"

1. URL (https://youtu.be/IMWga6vOf_o) "Too Tired Tonight"

Chorus:

"Because I'm too tired tonight, I can't put up a fight
You'll have to take what you can get from me
And if you don't find me pleasin' you ought to know the reason
This working life has stoled my energy"

"When you finish shaving, you want to bring me higher
Awake with loves ol' passion and kindle loves ol' fire
Your lookin' good in your pajamas, I'm what you're lookin' for
Wanna play with baby's momma, but I can't go no more"

"I hope that you don't scold me, but try to understand
I wish that I could hold you and respond to your command
But I'm afraid my getup has gotten up and went
And now I find my love's desire has nearly all been spent"

As the crowd shows their approval by applauding, Jeff approaches Phil Hurley, who is known to have contacts with a local recording studio. He informs Phil that he has just completed writing a few songs and that he would like to record, or at least have them recorded by a known professional.

Phil says, "I would like to hear you perform one of the songs here at the Inn." Jeff has performed songs in the past that have been made popular by other artist, but he has never claimed to have created his own material. Believing that the stranger lying in bed at the General Hospital will not survive, Jeff decides to proceed with his devious plan.

Arrangements are made with the MC to have Phil's request granted. Jeff is given the opportunity to show Phil what he can do

as he stands at the mike and announces, "this is a song I have just
completed. It's about a guy, Billy Credit, who relies on credit for
surviving from day to day. "

> [1]"Country singers come and go, they lose their selling power
> In the years of eternity, their fame is just an hour
> With names like Cash and Paycheck, what else would you expect
> Depression's here but I'll survive my name is Billy Credit
> Cash don't last long, paychecks always gone, you never can
> rely on them to get it
> There is only one who can sing a country song, inflation's
> here but I'll survive
> My Name is Billy Credit
>
> I keep expecting some to try, like Hank or Jimmy Bond
> I guess they don't cause they know they won't have a chance
> of lasting long
> It's true I'm sure, and what's more, I know someone has said it
> When you cash a bond, or paycheck's gone, you still have
> that ol' credit
> Cash don't last long, paycheck's always gone, you never can
> rely on them to get it There is only one who can sing a
> country song, depression's here but I'll survive My name is
> Billy credit
>
> Now we know there's money in a song that's on the charts
> I know how to get it there, I'll steal the women's hearts
> So if you want to start a band and get someone to head it
> You can keep the money son, the sweet things want the credit
> Cash don't last long, paycheck's always gone, you never can
> rely on them to get it
> There is only one who can sing a country song, inflation's
> here but I'll survive
> My name is Bill Credit."

The crowd applauds and Jeff is thinking that he wants to show
Phil his versatility. He asks everyone, "If you'll permit me, I'd like
to do one more of my numbers. It's called "Cloudy With a Good

Chance of Showers." Jeff tells the band to shift to a slow beat and, with a softer voice, begins to sing.

1. URL (https://youtu.be/Qav9ikwEa6Y) "Billy Credit"

[1]"Alone in the evenin' watching the TV, passing the lonely hours
We're not together, just watching the weather
It's cloudy with a god chance of showers
Cloudy with a good chance of showers, that's what the weather man says
Cloudy with a good chance of showers, this could go on for days

When we were together, I recall that I brought you, love kisses and flowers
But now I feel, just like the weather
It's cloudy with a good chance of showers
Cloudy with a good chance of showers, that's what the weather man says
Cloudy with a good chance of showers, this could go on for days

When we were together, nothing could harm us, living in ivory towers
But everything changes, just like the weather
Now it's cloudy with a good chance of showers
Cloudy with a good chance of showers, that's what the weather man says
Cloudy with a good chance of showers, this could go on for days

All this has left me, feeling so helpless, it seems I've lost all my powers
Never to walk again in the sunshine
It's cloudy with a good chance of showers, It's cloudy with a good chance of showers"

Jeff thanks the audience and steps down from the stage. Over the applause of the crowd, Phil tells Jeff that he may have something going with these songs. They make plans to meet and go over the remaining songs that, unbeknown to Phil, are supposedly written by Jeff. Jeff and Ruth leave the Red Fox in a state of euphoric anticipation of the future. They are unaware that Lora is in the process of loading her car as she completes her plans to drive to Nashville and be at Mark's bedside.

1. URL (https://youtu.be/4u5kFJnaPmk) "Cloudy with a Good Chance of Showers"

CHAPTER VII

Music Therapy

Lora arrives in Nashville and immediately goes to the General Hospital. A meeting with Mark's doctor, Dr. Warren, confirmed that his condition is critical. Lora says that she wants to be at Mark's side and do whatever possible to awaken him from his comatose state. She asks the Dr. Warren "would it help if I played some of the original songs that I have copied before leaving Cincinnati." The doctor agreed that it would be comforting to a comatose person to hear familiar sounds that remind them of a happier time.

It fact, Dr. Warren continues, the mind is capable of creating images, that we refer to as dreams, that ignore the actual sequence of events in time. It rearranges the events in order to integrate the actual sounds that are occurring into a meaningful series of events. This is helpful to a person who is comatose. It helps them to make sense of their surroundings while they're in this strange state.

Lora takes leave of the doctor and goes to the nurses' station, as directed. She meets Mark's nurse, Betty Walker, and explains that she will be staying with Mark. Betty takes Lora to Mark's room and helps her to settle in.

Lora begins to talk to Mark in a soft voice and reminisces about the good times that they have shared. "If only I could motivate you to come back to me so we could continue our lives", Lora says to Mark. She goes on, "I will remain by your side until you are able to travel down loves ol' road with me. I love you Mark."

With that, Lora sits back and begins to play a series of the songs they have recorded together at the Homestead. She is hoping that Mark can hear the song, "Sport," that is presently playing and that he will soon respond by awakening.

The song should help Mark to recall his relationship with his Grandfather's hound dog. It begins playing,

1I was roamin' the hills with a hound dog named Sport His spirit so deep and I found, it was there that I learned The true lesson's of life, let nobody's spirit be bound

> Then came the day, I went away and never to return
> Big town's a callin', I had to go, other lessons of life I must learn
> Here Sport! Here boy! Ho! Ho! If I could see my ol' friend
> Here Sport! Here boy! Ho! Ho! If I could just see him again
>
> The passing of time brought me to school, to read and forget about him
> The things they teach, I don't want to know, I think He's much wiser than them
>
> Some folks might say I've done very well, for me and my family
> But I wish that my son could run with that dog, and ol' Sport could teach him like me.
> Here Sport! Here boy! Ho! Ho! If I could see my ol' friend
> Here Sport! Here boy! Ho! Ho! If I could just see him again.

Lora continues to play through the series of recordings hoping that somehow it is helping Mark to fight for his recovery.

At this time, Betty enters the room and, as she checks on Mark, she cannot help but to hear the music that Lora is playing. Betty comments that, "the music is good but I don't believe that I have ever heard that song." Then Lora explains that, "it is one of the many songs that Mark has written." Betty completes her task and returns to the nurses' station.

1. URL (https://youtu.be/PZWWtxE6pLA) "Sport"

CHAPTER VIII

The Secret Revealed

Ruth Beckman walks by the desk were Betty is filling out the latest patient report on Mark. They begin to make small talk. Betty remarks about hearing one of the original song that Mark has written. She explains to Ruth that Lora has an entire series of songs that she is playing to encourage Mark to recover. When Betty starts reciting some of the words to Mark's song, a strange feeling comes over Ruth, and she is haunted by the similarity to one of creations that is claimed by her friend, Jeff.

Ruth decides to investigate for herself the music that is playing in Mark's room. She wants to be convinced that there is no relation between what Lora is playing and those claimed to be written by Jeff. On the pretense of checking the bathroom facilities, Ruth listens as Lora plays one of the songs, "The Juke Box Is Quite," that she had performed some time ago with Mark's band at the Homestead. Ruth listens closely to hear,

> [1]"It's not the darkest of hair, or the bluest of eyes
> That takes my man from my side.
> It's not the lure of a smile and I realize
> He has no other to hide
>
> (Chorus)

There is no woman who can compete with what he's needing
tonight
So he's there all alone, and I know he'll come home
When their closed and the juke box is quite

1. URL (https://youtu.be/PfpJEPZBwxc) "Juke Box Is Quite"

Though I may never know just what makes him run
Or just what goes on in his head
It's not a longing to kiss a stranger for fun
That keeps my man from our bed

Each night I'm saying a prayer for his safe return
And the day that he'll stay here with me Until then he will
go and know my concern In time is he going to see"

Ruth, is now certain that this is the same song that her friend is claiming to have written. She must decide how to approach this situation and believes that Mark's survival is key to what action she should take. If Jeff continues to have Phil promote his ill gained songs and Mark survives his injury's, then Jeff could be in a world of trouble. On the other hand, if Mark does not pull through then it is one word against the other as to whom this property belongs. Ruth thinks that no one is likely to take on the financial burden of defending Mark posthumously.

The fact remains that Mark has not yet succumbed to his injuries. This leads Ruth to wait until Mark's outcome is known before she tries to warn Jeff of the dangers of proceeding with his plans. She only hopes that Mark's condition will be revealed before Jeff has passed the point of no return.

CHAPTER IX

The Awakening

MEANWHILE, LORA CONTINUES HER mission of using musical therapy in hopes of returning Mark to the conscience world. She is presently exposing Mark to his song entitled "West Tennessee." It was written when Mark attended a technical seminar at the University of TN—At Martin. Mark can hear, but not respond to,

> [1]"I know that you've all be down to Knoxville And I know you've been on the Nashville scene But if you want the best, just move it further west To West TN, that's what I mean.
>
> (Chorus)
>
> "West TN, Oh West TN, the place that I'm proud to be from
> We ain't got the bright lights but we have the right life
> In West TN, and that's my home.
>
> It's a long way from Memphis north to Martin
> And many friendly towns are in between
> And in the western skies, with eagles soaring high
> You can almost hear those freedom bells ring

And if you want to raise your family
In a place where you know they'll see the light
Just come and settle down, in any little town
And in time you will find that you've done right"

1. URL (https://youtu.be/I6-kE0uwNH8) "West TN"

As the song ends, Mark's nurse enters the room and proceeds to perform her periodic examination of his condition. She notices that Mark is showing signs of conscience behavior. His eyes seem to be focusing on the surroundings and his fingers are slightly flexing. The nurse, in a state of excitement, tells Lora that Mark may be responding to the environment. The two agree to have the doctor notified immediately.

Dr. Warren confirms that Mark is no longer comatose and he will survive his ordeal. Lora is relieved and in a state of euphoria. She can hardly wait to see

Mark in his normal condition. "Dr. Warren cautions Lora by saying, Mark remains in a sensitive state and requires a good dose of rest. It is now a matter of allowing time to heal the damage that Mark has endured."

The word travels fast around the nurse's station and Ruth becomes aware of the recent development. She realizes that she must warn Jeff not have Phil to represent the ill-gotten property. In fact, Jeff must own up to his devious plan to steal Mark's songs before he winds up in even more trouble. It is not too late to prevent Jeff from paying a high price for his intentions.

CHAPTER X

Truth Prevails

RUTH CALLS JEFF AT his duty desk and informs him of the developments that have occurred at the Hospital. She insists that he corrects the situation before he gets in over his head. Since Jeff recalls that Mark had performed at the Red Fox Inn, he argues, "Mark could have stolen the songs from me while he was at the Red Fox a few months ago."

Finally, Ruth convinces Jeff that the cards are stacked against him. She says, "there are too many witness in the Cincinnati area that Mark can call on to substantiate his claims. You must admit to Phil that you have not been forthcoming about these songs."

Jeff relents and says, "ok, I will admit to Phil that I have been underhanded and that my unsavory action was driven by my ambition to make it in the music world."

Phil is contacted and Jeff relates the entire story to him. He tells Phil that he has in his possession a complete series of recordings of Mark's songs. Jeff further sates that he will help in any way possible to promote the songs. Phil asks Jeff to "forward the recordings to me and I will do my best to have a friend to broadcast one, or more, on the local radio station. "

After receiving the recordings, Phil visits his DJ friend at WSFC and induces him to give Mark's songs some consideration.

CHAPTER XI

A New Beginning

A WEEK, OR MORE, HAS passed since the conversation between Phil and Jeff. Back at the hospital, Dr. Warren is in Mark's room and trying to decide if his patient is well enough to be released from his care. Mark seems to be very aware of his surroundings and says, "I'll be alright if time will heal my broken ribs and leg."

Lora assures the doctor that she will see that Mark gets home safely and that she will care for him until he returns to a healthy state. With that, Dr. Warren agrees to release Mark into Lora's care. They proceed to pack Lora's car, leave the hospital and head up I-65 toward Cincinnati.

The two are reflecting on their recent experiences and wondering if anything will become of Mark's music. Even if the music business never works out, Mark feels that he still has a future in engineering. One way or another he will complete his PhD program at UC. It would be too much to expect that his interest in both music and technology would pay off.

As they are driving along, Mark turns on the radio to hear,

> [1]"If ya wanna know, I'll tell ya so 'bout life and love and pain
> 'Bout bummin' in the afternoon and sleepin' in the rain
> But for the likes of me, I cannot see and never will know why
> When they begin, the good things end, but the bad things multiply

Yes, I will never, never know why, when they begin the good things end but the bad things multiply.

1. URL (https://youtu.be/yCRaQNOfb7I) "If Ya Wanna Know"

There are things that change our way of life, the old folks used to say
You can't count on tomorrow, it's never like today
The good things change to bad times, so what they say is true
And the best time that I ever had was making love to you
Yes, the good times change to bad times, so what they say is true, and the best time that I ever had was making love to you

So now I'm free but I'd rather be, with one to love again
To fill this empty heart of mine, and change this mood I'm in
But time and change go hand in hand, so I'm waitin' patiently
For the hands of time to clear the past and bring new love to me
Yes, I am waiting so patiently, for the hands of time to clear the past and bring new love to me."

www.ingramcontent.com/pod-product-compliance
Lightning Source LLC
Chambersburg PA
CBHW031950130726
47904CB00012B/1093